How the Elephant got his Trunk

Adapted by Sheila Lane and Marion Kemp

Illustrations by Sallie Alane Reason

Take Part Starters

Level 1

Ⓦ **Ward Lock Educational Co. Ltd.**

Ward Lock Educational Co. Ltd.
BIC Ling Kee House
1, Christopher Road
East Grinstead
West Sussex
RH19 3BT

A member of the Ling Kee Group
London • New York • Hong Kong • Singapore

© Sheila Lane and Marion Kemp
This edition published 1989
Reprinted 1997
ISBN 0 7062 5116 4

Printed in Hong Kong

Contents

★ This sign means that you can make the sounds which go with the story.

Little Elephant and Giraffe

In this part of the story you will read about:

Little Elephant, who has a flat, bulgy nose and is always asking questions,

and Giraffe, who is always spanking Little Elephant with his hard, hard hoof.

Little Elephant is being spanked by his relations because he asks rude questions. ★

Giraffe   ★That's for asking your Aunt Hippopotamus why she is so fat.

Little Elephant   Ow! ★ Ow! ★

Giraffe   ★ And that's for asking your Uncle Gorilla why his eyes are so red.

Little Elephant   Ow! ★ Ow! ★

Giraffe   ★ And that's for asking your Aunt Ostrich why her tail feathers stick out.

Little Elephant   Ow! ★ Ow! ★

Giraffe   ★ And THAT'S for asking ME why I am so spotty.

Little Elephant   OW! ★ NO! ★

Giraffe   Now, listen to me, Little Elephant! . . . Are you listening?

Little Elephant	Yes! I'm listening.
Giraffe	Do you want your relations to stop spanking you?
Little Elephant	Yes, I do!
Giraffe	Then you must stop asking them rude questions about what they look like. Do you hear?
Little Elephant	Yes, I hear.
Giraffe	In fact, you'd better not ask any questions at all. Do you hear?
Little Elephant	Yes, I hear.
Giraffe	So, STOP ASKING QUESTIONS, or . . .
Little Elephant	Or . . . what?

Giraffe Or . . . the C . . . R . . . O . . . C . . . O . . . D . . . I . . . L . . . E . . . will get you.

Little Elephant WHAT IS the C . . . R . . . O . . . C . . . O . . . D . . . I . . . L . . . E . . . ?

Giraffe DON'T ASK QUESTIONS!

Little Elephant But . . . WHAT IS IT ?

Giraffe I told you not to ask questions!
★ Take that! ★ And that!

Little Elephant OW! ★ OW! ★

Giraffe And stop making a noise!
Do you hear?

Little Elephant I hear . . .
BUT . . .

Giraffe But . . . WHAT?

Little Elephant	Oh . . . NOTHING!
Giraffe	Listen, Little Elephant, and I'll tell you something important.
Little Elephant	Yes?
Giraffe	It's bad luck . . . VERY BAD LUCK even to whisper the C . . . R . . . O . . . C . . . O . . . D . . . I . . . L . . . E . . . 's name. So you must NEVER say it. Never, NEVER, N E V E R!
Little Elephant	But I want to know what . . . IT . . . looks like.
Giraffe	I said, 'NO QUESTIONS!' ★ Take that!
Little Elephant	OW! ★ But I want to know where IT lives.
Giraffe	I said, 'NO QUESTIONS!' ★ Take THAT! ★
Little Elephant	OW! ★ AND I want to know what IT has for dinner.

Giraffe   Well . . . I did warn you!

Little   OW! ★ OW! ★ OW! ★
Elephant I'm not stopping here!

Giraffe   Oh! So where are you going?

Little   I'm going to find the
Elephant C . . . R . . . O . . . C . . .
O . . . D . . . I . . . L . . . E . . . !

Little Elephant and Bird

In this part of the story you will read about:

Little Elephant,   and Bird.

Little Elephant is running through the trees
when he sees Bird sitting in a thorn bush. ★

Bird Hello, Little Elephant!

Little Elephant Hello, Bird!

Bird Where are your mother and father on this fine day?

Little Elephant At home.

Bird And where are all your relations?

Little Elephant At home.

Bird Are you all alone in the forest, Little One?

Little Elephant Yes.

Bird Then may I ask what you are doing?

Little Elephant I'm looking for the C . . . R . . . O . . . C . . . O . . . D . . . I . . . L . . . E . . . !

Bird Ah! You mean the . . . CROC — O — DILE.

Little So that's what IT is . . .
Elephant the CROC — O — DILE!

Bird Yes, that's right . . . CROCODILE! But are you sure you want to find the Crocodile, Little One ?

Little Yes! I want to know what it looks like.
Elephant

Bird Is there anything else you want to know about the Crocodile?

Little Yes, Bird!
Elephant I want to know where it lives.

Bird Anything else?

Little And I want to know what it has for dinner.
Elephant

Bird Have you asked your relations to tell you about the Crocodile, Little One?

Little Yes, but they won't!
Elephant

Bird Then I can't tell you.

Little Elephant Oh, please tell me, Bird. Please! PLEASE!

Bird Well — I'll tell you where to go and then you can find one for yourself.

Little Elephant Oooh! Where do I go?

Bird To the Limpopo River! Go to the banks of the GREAT-GREY-GREEN-GREASY LIMPOPO RIVER and FIND OUT!

13

Little Elephant and Rock Snake

In this part of the story you will read about:

Little Elephant,   and Rock Snake.

On his way to the Limpopo River, Little Elephant meets Rock Snake, who is curled round a rock. ★

Rock Snake	Hello, Little Elephant!
Little Elephant	Hello, Rock Snake!
Rock Snake	Where's your family on this fine day?
Little Elephant	At home.
Rock Snake	Oh! And where are all your relations?
Little Elephant	They are at home too.
Rock Snake	So what are you doing here, may I ask?
Little Elephant	I'm looking for the Crocodile.
Rock Snake	The . . . WHAT?
Little Elephant	The Crocodile.

Rock Snake	Tell me something, Little Elephant! Why do you want to find the Crocodile?
Little Elephant	I want to know what it has for dinner.
Rock Snake	Pss! Pss! You can't want to know that!
Little Elephant	Yes, I do!
Rock Snake	Pss! Pss! And where do you think you will find the Crocodile?
Little Elephant	In the river!
Rock Snake	Pss! PSS! Do you mean the GREAT-GREY-GREEN-GREASY-LIMPOPO River?
Little Elephant	Yes!
Rock Snake	Listen to old Rock Snake, Little One! GO HOME — NOW!

Little Elephant	No!
Rock Snake	What you need, Little Elephant, is a good spanking! Hasn't anyone ever told you that?
Little Elephant	Yes! Lots of times!
Rock Snake	Well, I think I'll give you one! ★ Take that! ★ And that!
Little Elephant	Ow! Ow!
Rock Snake	Now off you go HOME!
Little Elephant	NO! I'm going to find the Crocodile! ★

Little Elephant and Crocodile

In this part of the story you will read about:

Little Elephant,   and the Crocodile.

Little Elephant is standing on the bank of the Limpopo River, looking at SOMETHING floating in the water.

Crocodile   Hello, Little One!

Little   Who are you?
Elephant

Crocodile   Don't you KNOW who I am?

Little   No!
Elephant

Crocodile   Never mind! Tell me what you're doing here,
Little One.

Little   I'm looking for someone.
Elephant

Crocodile   And who is that someone, I wonder?

Little   THE CROCODILE!
Elephant   Have you seen it?

Crocodile   Have I seen . . . IT?!
Ho, ho ho!
I AM the Crocodile!

Little Elephant	So YOU are the CROCODILE! Let me look at you.
Crocodile	Look at me for as long as you like.
Little Elephant	I've been looking for you for days and days and days.
Crocodile	Well, here I am! So . . . what can I do for you?
Little Elephant	Well . . . I DID want to know what you look like.
Crocodile	And now you know! Anything else?
Little Elephant	And I DID want to know where you live.
Crocodile	And now you know! Anything else?
Little Elephant	YES!
Crocodile	Ask me, then.

Little Elephant	I want to know . . . what you have for dinner.
Crocodile	Come closer, Little One, and I'll whisper.
Little Elephant	Yes!
Crocodile	Closer . . . CLOSER . . . C L O S E R . . .!
Little Elephant	Yes!

Crocodile	I think . . . I think . . . today I'll begin with . . . LITTLE ELEPHANT!
Little Elephant	Ow! OW! O W! LET . . . ME . . . GO!
Crocodile	Let you go — not likely! I've got you . . . and I'm going to keep you!
Little Elephant	NO! NO! N O! LET . . . ME . . . GO!
Crocodile	NO! I've got you by your little nose . . . and I'll . . . PULL IT . . . and PULL IT . . .!

Little Elephant   LET . . . ME . . . GO!

Crocodile   NO!

Little Elephant   LET . . . ME . . . GO!

Crocodile   N . . . N . . . n . . . no!

Little Elephant   ROCK SNAKE! ROCK SNAKE!
HOLD ON TO ME!
PULL ROCK SNAKE! P U L L! ★
That's it!
He's let go!
OWW! My nose!

Little Elephant and Rock Snake

In this part of the story you will read about:

Little Elephant,

and Rock Snake.

Rock Snake is fanning Little Elephant's sore trunk nose with a banana leaf. ★

Rock Snake Stop crying, Little One! Sss! Sss! I'll fan your poor hot nose with this banana leaf.

Little Elephant ★ Ow! Ow!

Rock Snake Sss! Sss! You've got a long trunk nose now, and no mistake!

Little Elephant ★ Ow! Ow!
My poor nose is so hot!

Rock Snake You're lucky to have a nose at all, Little One! If I hadn't saved you . . .

Little Elephant Oh, yes!
You saved me, Rock Snake.
You saved me from the Crocodile.

Rock Snake Now you know what the Crocodile would like to have for dinner!

Little Elephant Yes! Little Elephant!

Rock Snake Sss! Dip your hot nose into the pool, Little One.

Little Elephant Ooo! Ooo!

Rock Snake Is your poor nose beginning to feel lovely and cool now?

Little Elephant Ooo! Yes! It's lovely and cool.

Rock Snake Sss! Sss-stretch your long trunk nose up to those bananas, Little One.

Little Elephant Like that?

Rock Snake Yes-sss! Now pick yourself a ripe banana.

Little Elephant Look! Look! I've got it!

Rock Snake Sss-so! You couldn't have done that with your old, flat nose, could you?

Little Elephant	No!
Rock Snake	Do you think you're beginning to like this new nose of yours, Little One ?
Little Elephant	Well . . . yes . . . ! OW! ★ OW! ★
Rock Snake	Pss! Pss! What's the matter now?
Little Elephant	OW! It's a fly!
Rock Snake	Hit it with that long trunk nose of yours. Go on!
Little Elephant	★ GOT IT!

Rock Snake   You couldn't have done
that with your old,
flat nose, Little One!

Little   Look at me now,
Elephant   Rock Snake!★

Rock Snake   Yes-sss! SSS-slap that lovely, cool, sss-sloshy
mud all over your hot little head.

Little   Ooo! Yes!
Elephant   I like mud! ★ It's lovely and cool.

Rock Snake   Could you have done that with your old, flat
nose, Little One?

Little   No! I couldn't!
Elephant

Rock Snake	Liss-sss-ten, Little One! Don't you think the time has come for you to go home to all your relations?
Little Elephant	No! Not yet!
Rock Snake	What's the matter? Don't you want your relations to start spanking you again?
Little Elephant	NO!
Rock Snake	Lis-sss-ten, Little One! How would YOU like to start spanking YOUR relations?
Little Elephant	ME!
Rock Snake	Yes-sss — YOU! You'll find that long trunk of yours very useful for spanking people!
Little Elephant	Ooo! YES! OOO! I'm not stopping here! I'm going home! ★

Little Elephant and Giraffe Again

In this part of the story you will read about:

Little Elephant,

and Giraffe.

Little Elephant is showing his long trunk nose to all his relations.

Giraffe	Good gracious! What HAS happened to your nose, Little Elephant?
Little Elephant	It's been pulled!
Giraffe	Well! This long, trunk nose you've got now is very ugly.
Little Elephant	I like it.
Giraffe	But — where did you get it from?
Little Elephant	The Crocodile!
Giraffe	The . . . the . . . the . . . CR . . . Didn't I tell you that it's bad luck . . . VERY BAD LUCK . . . even to whisper that name ? Didn't I tell you never, never, NEVER to . . .
Little Elephant	Crocodile . . . CROCODILE . . . C R O C O D I L E!
Giraffe	COME HERE! You bad Little Elephant! I'm going to SPANK YOU!

Little Elephant	Oh no, you're not! I'm going to spank YOU! ★
Giraffe	OW! OW! STOP! STOP!
Little Elephant	No, I won't stop! ★ Take that! ★ AND THAT!
Giraffe	GO AWAY, Little Elephant! Go away and take all your Elephant family with you. Take them to the GREAT-GREY-GREEN-GREASY-LIMPOPO RIVER and get new noses for them from the . . . CR . . .
Little Elephant	CROCODILE!

So that's what they did! AND FROM THAT TIME TO THIS DAY ALL THE ELEPHANTS YOU WILL EVER SEE HAVE LONG TRUNK NOSES . . . JUST LIKE LITTLE ELEPHANT'S.